WITHDRAWN
WILLIAMSBU
D0696079

R.F. KRISTI

THE DIARY OF A SNOOPY CAT

Illustrated by Jorge Valle

(WITH CONTRIBUTIONS TO THE CARTOONS BY VIDEO EXPLAINER)

WILLIAMSBURG REGIONAL LIBRARY
7770 CROAKER ROAD
WILLIAMSBURG, VA 23188

JAN - - 2020

QUIZ TIME:

Connect via:

www.incabookseries.com

If you enjoy this book, please leave a review on
Amazon or Goodreads.
Positive reviews help a great deal.

Thank you

LEGAL NOTICE

COPYRIGHT © 2017 BY R.F. KRISTI
WWW.INCABOOKSERIES.COM

NO PART OF THIS WORK MAY BE TRANSMITTED
OR REPRODUCED BY ANY MEANS OR IN ANY
FORMAT, ELECTRONIC OR MECHANICAL, INCLUDING
RECORDING OR PHOTOCOPYING OR USING ANY
FORM OF MANUAL REPRODUCTION, OR WITH ANY
INFORMATION STORAGE/RETRIEVAL SYSTEM,
WITHOUT OBTAINING PRIOR WRITTEN PERMISSION
FROM THE PUBLISHER OF THIS WORK.

PLEASE SEND REQUESTS FOR FURTHER
INFORMATION OR PERMISSION TO COPY ALL OR
PARTS OF THIS WORK TO THE PUBLISHER.

PUBLISHED BY: R.F. KRISTI
(WWW.INCABOOKSERIES.COM) -
FIRST EDITION

Copyright © 2017 R.F. Kristi
All rights reserved.
ISBN:
ISBN

ACKNOWLEDGEMENTS
TO

My mentor Alinka Rutkowska for her motivational guidance.

My editor Amithy Moragoda Alles for her inspiration & attention to detail.

My illustrator Jorge Valle for his talent in bringing the Inca series to life - in the most wonderful manner.

&

The team at Video Explainer for their contribution to the cartoons.

THANK YOU

My "Family Tree"

Take A Peek @ My Family:

INCA (ME):

I am a Siberian kitty, and we Siberians are a pretty good-looking bunch.

I am the natural leader of the Troupe.

There are several reasons for this.

After all,

* ❖ I am the eldest and the BIG sis of the furry pack!
* ❖ I am a super smart kitty!

I bet you, you wouldn't find any kitty smarter than me, even if you swam all the way to China. Mom does not know it, but I AM the TOPSTER around here.

CARA:

Cara, a Siamese kitty, is my pretty sister.

She is the prissy one in our family.

She is always well-groomed, prim and proper and very attached to Mom.

She is mom's pet. She can do no wrong in Mom's eyes and Cara loves to suck up to her. **Ugh!**

FROMAGE:

My brother Fromage is a Tabby-cat. Fromage was named after the French cheese he adores, as fromage means cheese in French.

Fromage loves cheese, any type of cheese, period. He also considers himself a great cheese expert.

Fromage is the mascot of our cheese shop. He goes to the shop with Mom every day. He has built himself a following in the cheese loving circles of London.

He strongly believes that our cheese shop is a triumph because of him.

Fromage is also accident-prone and in the habit of getting into all types of scrapes. If you find something broken in our household, you can bet your bottom dollar that Fromage was behind it!

CHARLOTTE:

Charlotte is a Roborovski dwarf hamster and Fromage's best buddy.

She had met Fromage in our cheese shop in Paris and decided to come with us to London.

Charlotte is devoted to Fromage despite the number of pickles he gets himself into. I don't understand this friendship between Fromage and Charlotte. Charlotte is intelligent and sharp. Whereas, Fromage is??? Well, Fromage is Fromage.

Fromage likes to yap non-stop and Charlotte likes to listen. This may be the main reason why they are good friends.

Fromage gets jealous if anyone tries to become too friendly with Charlotte.

MISSY (MOM):

Mom is a humanoid jointly owned by us.

The humanoids call her Missy, but she is Mom to us kitties.

Mom runs our cheese shop. The cheese shop is situated in the heart of Kensington. It is modeled on our successful cheese shop in Paris.

We let Mom get away with thinking that she owns us, when it is us kitties who actually own Mom.

Our world revolves around Mom, but she has a bee in her bonnet about things that we kitties never care about.

❖ Our food

Our diet is carefully controlled by Mom much against our wishes.

No amount of twirling and meowing around her feet can change her mind when she prepares dinner. Even looking at her with adoring eyes gets us nowhere.

Drat!!!! Drat!!!! & Treble Drat!!!

Mom's NO! NO! Food List for us Kitties

No cream
No bacon
No ice-cream
No pizza

No good stuff!!!!!!

❖ Our cleanliness

Mom is a clean freak! When we least expect it – out come our fur cleaning brushes.

Fromage tries to hide as soon as she gets out our brushes.

But Cara puts on her prissy look and actually purrs when Mom brushes her, her blue eyes blinking like two glorious sapphires - aimed solely at Mom.

Fromage usually snarls "traitor" at her as he dashes under the sofa.

But does she care?

NOoooooo!

I pretend to protest too, but I can't help liking the brush strokes on my fur. In any case, you can't stop Mom when she gets into her "clean the kitties" mood.

So why not enjoy it?

AUNT FLORENCE:

Aunt Florence is Mom's humanoid Aunt.

I am not shy to say that Aunt Florence dotes on me.

She is the only family Mom has apart from us. Aunt Florence used to live in the cottage we occupy in Kensington, London. Aunt Florence now lives in Provence, France.

NOW THAT YOU HAVE HAD A PEEK AT MY FAMILY, LET'S GET TO THE EXCITING STUFF!!!

RAMBLE ...
RAMBLE ...
PREAMBLE

One Saturday Morning in early December:

My life was becoming SOooooo exciting!

It was about the time that I started writing a Diary!

You may ask - Why a Diary for a Puddy Kat??? - !!!

The reason is simple.

Since arriving in London from Paris with my family, I had been involved in my very first detective adventure.

From that time onwards, I had fantasized on becoming the world's smartest cat detective.

No. 1 Celebrity Snoopy Kitty in the World

Writing my Diary became important as I was on my way to making my dream a reality. Hence, what better way to keep track of my success stories other than recording my snoopy adventures?

I decided that I was already the best snoopy cat in London.

No doubt about that!

My fame would soon spread to other parts of the country and then beyond, even to my home town Paris in France.

I imagined my kitty friends in Paris hearing about the famous snoopy cat.

They would recognize me with wonder.

Some would say it was "meant to be" and recognize me as a super-duper detective cat – a detective cat 'par excellence!'

Others would be jealous and claim that it was "mere chance".

There was no doubt about it - even the jealous kitties would be forced to recognize a world-famous cat detective!

Sneaking an empty note-book from Mom's desk when she was not looking had been a breeze.

The adventures of Inca the Siberian wonder cat, the best-known detective kitty in the planet, would become a masterpiece --- A sure hit --- A best-seller!

Who could resist snoopy kitty stories such as mine?

Yes --- my detective powers would get me on the road to stardom.

The time was right to get started as Christmas was around the corner. There was a feeling of tingling excitement in the air.

No doubt about it! Christmas was my favorite time of the year. The smell of pine trees, the shiny decorations and most of all our presents under the twinkling stars of our Christmas tree.

I had told Cara and Fromage about my Diary and all they wanted to know was how important **their** role would be in my Diary.

"Let's see," was all I would promise.

I heard a murmur of "smarty pants" from Cara that I pretended to ignore.

This was MY Diary and I would decide what I write in it.

So there!!!

Smarty pants, indeed!

No way was I going to let my sis and bro take over my Diary. I could imagine what it would become:

- ❖ From Fromage – Long rigamarole about his wonderful French cheese!!!!
- ❖ From Cara – The latest in scarves and how to make yourself pretty!!!!!

I imagined, in a dreamy state, a crowd of doggies bowing to my superior intelligence.

YESSS!

I would be Inca, the detective cat par excellence!

Never would a cat be SOOOOO adored by the masses.

Bravo! Inca

DECEMBER

12 Days Before Christmas

Sunday, Late Evening:

I suddenly had a strange feeling that we were being watched.

Missy our Mom had lit a fire in the fireplace and the wood was crackling brightly. The cottage was warm and cozy despite the cold outside.

It was a typical evening in the Inca household. Cara, Fromage, Charlotte and I were seated around the fireplace with Mom, the young humanoid we jointly owned.

Thinking I was imagining being watched, I shook my head and settled down.

The strange feeling of being watched crept back again.

Not wanting to disturb the others, I cautiously peered out of the window. There was nothing there - just darkness with a little light from the large luminous moon overhead.

I circled around on the same spot and settled down again with my face turned towards the window, just in case ALIENS from outer-space attacked us through the window.

Just as my eyes started to close, I saw a shadow moving outside the window. I opened my eyes wide and looked. But there was nothing there. Just the stillness of a very dark night.

Suddenly, I caught sight of two shiny green eyeballs staring at me.

My heart stood still!

* Was it a demon?
* Was it a fire-eating dragon??
* Was it a slithering serpent???

❖ Was my greatest fear about to become a reality? Were the Aliens out to get us????

My heart started beating wildly going –

I saw a strong, big, gray paw stretching out towards me and the fur on the back of my neck rose like a porcupine ready for battle.

Then it dawned on me that the portly figure in the window, appearing and disappearing, was only the face of our friend Monk!!

I let out a slow breath and my heart gradually returned to a normal rhythmic beat.

Monk, a Blue Russian cat with long legs and large golden-green eyes was rather handsome and sleek - if you go for the chunky type. He always sported a bright, red, bow-tie.

Monk was a pretty clever kitty.

Don't get me wrong. Most cats are naturally intelligent. But I had noted that Monk was far brainier than most of the kitties I had met. I suppose you could call him a NERDY cat.

Monk lived next door to us with Solo (a world-famous detective), his assistant Hobbs, and Terrance a big dog.

Terrance was Monk's best friend and a great doggie-detective himself.

I got up slowly so as not to disturb the others, leaped out of the window and joined Monk under the thick shrub separating our cottage from the sprawling garden in front of his large house.

"What's up Monk?" I softly purred.

The calm and easy-going Monk looked pretty shaken.

My ears tingled and the fur on the back of my neck that had flattened, once again pricked up when I sensed how upset he was.

"You OK?" I meowed, beating down my own panic.

Monk gulped and responded in his usual unhurried meow making an effort to squash his alarm.

"You kitties have to come over tonight. Terrance has some unexpected news for us," he murmured.

I promised him that we would, as soon as Mom fell asleep.

I hurried back to the others to break the news, wondering what was troubling the usually calm Monk.

Sunday Night:

The night was pitch black when we scampered over to Monk's home. Compared to our small and modest cottage, Monk lived in a huge and fancy house. But we loved our little cottage and wouldn't change it for anything in the world.

We padded across the great kitchen, with Fromage stopping to sniff at the tempting plate of cream left for Monk by Hobbs.

"Come on Fromage," Cara hissed. "Monk will not be too pleased if you dig into his snack without asking him."

"No way Cara, Monk is my pal!" responded Fromage as he stuck out his tongue at Cara.

He followed us nevertheless, looking back longingly at the full plate of cream.

Monk and Terrance were sitting together in a warm room, in front of a huge fireplace where the wood was still crackling.

At first, I had been surprised by Monk's friendship with Terrance.

How could a smart cat like Monk be so pally with a dog?

Then I had got to know Terrance myself, and I was forced to change my mind.

We kitties had a poor opinion of dogs. But Terrance was someone that even us cats had grown to like and respect.

To be honest, our opinion of doggies had slowly changed.

We had never moved around with doggies before arriving in London. We never wanted to either. We had treated them as dreadful furry beasts somewhat on the sniffy side.

It was different now. We had two good doggie friends that we hobnobbed with daily.

Terrance and Polo!

Terrance was a powerful dog, a golden retriever with long gold hair. He is one smart doggie despite his rather sappy grin and his pink, drooling, floppy tongue.

He was famous for having helped Solo solve many detective cases.

If there was one thing I respected, it was his popularity with both the animal kingdom and the two-legged humanoid friends around us.

Never mind his foolish grin and drooling tongue.

I could do with some of that popularity myself.

Terrance usually went everywhere with Solo and Hobbs.

Solo had sent Terrance to a well-known training school for dogs. Solo was not sorry to have done so as Terrance had topped his class at the Canine Search and Rescue academy. Terrance was a valuable partner in the detective agency headed by Solo.

I was impatient to find out what Terrance was up to now.

Terrance wagged his tail when he saw us and gave us a welcoming grin. Monk jumped up from his favorite chair and came to welcome us.

"Anyone wants some fresh cream?" he purred in his croaky meow.

"Thank you, NO," responded Cara before Fromage or I could get a word in, "we all had our dinner before coming."

Fromage glared at her.

Knowing my brother well and that he would get into a brawl right away, I quickly changed the subject.

"Terrance, what is going on?" I meowed.

"Some important news concerning Raoul, Polo's missing dad!" said Terrance once we had settled down in our usual places in the library.

I need to explain about Polo our pal and his sad family state.

Polo is a Pekinese doggie. He is short and just a tiny bit bigger than me.

We had got to know Polo when we moved to London from Paris in June this year. For some reason or other, he had developed a special place in his heart for Charlotte.

There had been some jealousy between Fromage and Polo over Charlotte. I was relieved that this was now ancient history.

Polo was owned by Señora Conchita Consoles, commonly known as the Señora, a popular opera singer, now retired.

The Señora had lost her husband Raoul who went missing while climbing Mount Everest in the Himalayas. She had been sad until we came on the scene.

She was slowly recovering from the loss of Raoul. But we knew that Polo and the Señora both missed Raoul terribly.

We had become good friends after we helped Polo during the mystery of the Señora's stolen diamond necklace.

The outcome had been surprising but fantastic, despite the anxiety of Fromage's disappearance and the discovery of the necklace in a very odd place.

It was at that time that I had been smitten by the detective bug. I longed to be involved in another case, and become a famous detective myself.

Terrance continued his story in short barks while we listened all agog.

"Solo brought home some news that would send Polo over the moon, if it turns out to be true.

"Solo has an old friend who works for Doctors Without Borders in Nepal.

"On a recent trip to London, the young doctor told Solo that he had heard of a foreigner, injured who was being cared for by some locals in a village near the Himalayas.

"From the brief description, Solo suspected that it maybe Señora's husband Raoul.

"We are going to the Himalayas to check this out since Solo is not sure if it is really Raoul, Polo's master.

"If either the Señora or Polo hears about this news and it turns out to be someone else, they would be really upset.

"What is most important is to keep this information from both the Señora and Polo until we are sure this foreigner is Raoul," said Terrance.

"Don't you worry; we will make sure that Polo never hears of this," I said giving Fromage and Charlotte a stern look.

"Never in my life would I wish to disappoint Polo. He is our friend," said Charlotte as she gave Fromage a beady look, her eyes narrowing.

"Me too," muttered Fromage sheepishly. I breathed a sigh of relief.

Terrance gave us further details.

He would accompany Solo and Hobbs to Nepal. They would travel by plane from England to Kathmandu, the capital city of Nepal, and then hire a car up to the Himalayas. From there they'd go on foot to the village with a local guide.

Terrance told us that the part on foot was dangerous and difficult. They had to trek along narrow mountainous slopes.

But Solo was determined to do this as Raoul was his good friend. If Raoul was alive, it would mean everything in the world for the Señora to be able to see him again.

"Not only the Señora," piped in Charlotte.

"It would be for Polo too. He adored Raoul! He is Polo's Dad after all" breathed Charlotte her little nose twitching.

We promised Terrance not to breath a word to Polo with regard to the reason they were leaving for Nepal.

"When will you leave?" I asked.

"Tomorrow," barked Terrance.

"Hobbs is getting our stuff ready. He has already bought the plane tickets for Nepal. I am going now for my vaccinations to travel out of the country."

A sudden thought crossed my mind - What about Christmas?

The plan had been for all of us to celebrate Christmas together at Solo's place. Señora, Polo, their housekeepers, the nice Applebee couple who were relatives of Hobbs, and Mom had been planning the Christmas dinner menu for weeks.

"If all goes well, we should be back by Christmas," said Terrance.

A sudden chill ran down my spine when I saw the thoughtful expression passing between the old friends, Monk and Terrance.

I remembered that Terrance had said that the latter part of the journey was very dangerous, even life-threatening.

Here I was with my thoughts about enjoying Christmas when Monk's family was going to be trekking through some of the most dangerous roads in the world in order to help Señora and Polo, two of our good friends.

How selfish of me!!

No wonder Monk had been in full panic mode when he visited me earlier.

He seemed to have calmed down now, but I suppose he was anxious about his family going on such a dangerous journey - wondering if they would come back safe.

The Himalayas! Hmm... I thought. I had not heard of this place before. I who normally liked to know everything was stumped.

"Where is this place?" I asked Terrance.

Terrance ran up to Solo's large writing table and brought us a booklet with pictures of the Himalayas.

What a breathtaking sight! Lots of mountains peaked with snow. The whole place looked huge and unfriendly. I could imagine how cold it would be there.

I pictured Terrance surveying the Himalayas, ready to conquer it.

"Solo does not consider this the best time of year to visit the Himalayas, as from November to March it is bitterly cold," barked Terrance.

"On the other hand, Solo doesn't wish to wait a moment longer in case Raoul is still alive and in need of medical help.

We are flying directly to Kathmandu," ended Terrance.

"Will it be hard living on your own, Monk?" asked Cara in her soft meow.

"Lance is coming over. Solo called him last night and asked him to house-sit here until they got back," replied Monk with a blink.

"Who is Lance?" asked Fromage.

"Lance is Solo's distant relative," said Monk.

"He is a young chap, always up to something or the other. He comes around when Solo and Hobbs go off on a case."

"He is ok but I try to stay out of his hair. He usually lolls around watching TV while stuffing his face and has some crazy ideas to raise money," meowed Monk.

11 Days Before Christmas

Monday Morning:

We hurried over to Monk's place to see our friends off to the Himalayas.

Solo and Hobbs had lots of luggage all laid out on the landing. They were taking their warm winter jackets and stout boots to keep them warm in the high elevation of the Himalayas.

Terrance himself had a warm fleece jacket and boots to protect his paws from jagged stones and cold weather.

There were also strong tents and a large box of canned goods to keep them all fed for two weeks.

Fresh food was to be bought in the local market, by the guide, before taking the long trek.

Terrance had his own canned food and a big packet of doggie croquettes.

Fromage had told me that when Mom heard that they were going, she had brought a huge chunk of French cheese, well wrapped in foil, for their journey.

He sniffed the cheese from the outside of the box and said that it was safely packed inside.

Monk scowled as his family was about to leave.

Knowing Monk well by now, I knew that he was troubled for their safety though he kept it well hidden. Nevertheless, his usual breezy good-natured face looked pinched.

"Keep strong buddy, we will be back before you notice that we are gone," said Terrance to Monk.

"Don't worry too much about Monk. I promise you that we will keep him company until you come back," I whispered to Terrance when Monk was not looking.

"Stay safe and bring everyone back and hopefully Raoul, too. That would make Polo a happy camper," I added.

"Thanks Inca. It was a lucky day when you all moved next door," barked Terrance as he gave me his quirky lopsided grin with his pink tongue hanging out.

A large black taxi pulled up soon after. Lance, who had arrived earlier, Hobbs and the taxi driver loaded the car with the luggage, and off they went on their journey to Nepal.

I turned from the doorway to take a look at Lance.

He was a sandy haired young chap with bright blue eyes. He was casually dressed in blue jeans and pullover and had an "I don't care" air about him.

Lance was inspecting Cara by carrying her high up in the air and from Cara's face I knew she did not like being carried by this stranger.

He then turned to me and lifted me up and carefully looked me over.

I wondered why the sudden interest in US while he had ignored Fromage completely.

I wriggled out of his arms and jumped down.

"How dare he carry me and inspect me as if I was a science specimen?" I thought to myself.

I had a feeling that Lance had something up his sleeve.

"Let's get back home," I said to the others, not wanting to be around Lance any longer than necessary.

After inviting Monk to come over and spend some time with us whenever he wished, we left Monk and Lance and raced back home as Mom would be returning home for dinner.

We loved racing one another. I am small in size, but I am quick too. I could beat both Cara and Fromage in getting my head through the door.

Fromage had decided not to go to the cheese shop that morning as he wished to say goodbye to Terrance.

Even one day away from his beloved cheese shop was too much for Fromage.

Monday Evening:

Mom was working on her laptop, sitting cross-legged on the comfy sofa.

Cara and Fromage had hogged the little mat in front of the fireplace, and Charlotte was settled comfortably on Fromage's woolen winter scarf.

I surveyed my family and yawned widely on the back of the sofa behind Mom. This was my preferred position as the head honcho of the

Inca kingdom. I also liked to read what Mom was typing away on the computer.

In the evenings Mom would write out the day's sales from the family cheese business. I always liked to keep an eye on how our business was going.

The weather had changed since the warm summer days, and we were spending the first days of December in our new cottage.

Although the weather had quickly turned cold, our little cottage was warm and toasty, the way we kitties liked it.

Suddenly Mom's Skype started playing a melody and Aunt Florence's face appeared on the screen.

I didn't move but my ears twitched to attention as the conversation turned to plans for Christmas.

Aunt Florence was coming to London for Christmas.

Hurray!!!

There were several reasons that Aunt Florence was a STAR in our household:

- ❖ I generally had Aunt Florence twisted around my paws. She spoiled me rotten and gave me lots of attention.
- ❖ Fromage loved her as Aunt Florence always sneaked in special treats for him when Mom was not looking.
- ❖ Cara loved her as she always made something special for her to wear.

All in all, Aunt Florence was a welcome visitor.

Just to get some attention I peered over Mom's shoulder so that Aunt Florence could see me. She blew me some kisses and I purred back loudly.

I could see myself in the little box on the screen and eyed myself while they chatted.

"Hmmm, not bad, not bad at all," I murmured to myself.

Yes, all intact. My soft, smoky, gray and white coat was well brushed and smooth. My magnificent tail fell gracefully like a plush velvet scarf.

I am a pretty unusual kitty, in addition to my spiffy looks.

I should mention at this point that I am blessed with telepathic powers. In other words, I have had quite some practice sending messages directly from my mind and receiving info from another's mind.

Naturally, it is with Mom that I practice this skill most often.

I studied my facial expression and tried one or two looks showing a famous cat detective.

A world-famous snoop must have a serious face, I thought to myself. I gazed at myself with a stern expression.

"All good," I murmured to myself on the screen, "and even if I say so myself, a good-looking kitty am I!"

Some fur balls in my household think I am a wee bit vain.

Oh well! no one can be purrrfect, can they?

Dragging my thoughts away from myself, I started thinking of Christmas.

Christmas is a fun-time! I wondered how it would be this year.

Aunt Florence always spent Christmas with us. But then we had been living in France.

After moving to London, we had made lots of new friends.

Surely this Christmas would also be great fun with so many more people?

Mom suddenly sat up and sniffed the air.

What was that?

I sat up too and wrinkled my nose, sniffing the air.

Sniff, sniff, sniff, sniff.

How come I hadn't noticed the strong smell slowly swamping our sitting room?

What was that terrible but familiar smell invading our living room?

Got it!!!!!

It was the strong smell of ripe old French cheese!

A great chunk of cheese hidden behind a painting was slowly melting and dripping down. The warm room was enveloped by the rich and overpowering smell of French cheese.

Drip, splat!

Drip, splat!

Drip, splat!

I dare you to guess who would have hidden this large piece of cheese!

Yep, you are right!

It was Fromage, of course!!

Who else could it be???

He had hidden a huge chunk of cheese for his midnight snack. The cheese was now fully melted due to the warmth of the fire that had been lit all evening.

"Pheeweee!!!!"

"What a smell!" Said Cara as she held her nose.

Mom cleaned up the mess with a stern warning to Fromage that he should not help himself to cheese from the shop when no one was watching.

Fromage was all upset. Not about stealing the cheese, but because his wonderful cheese had melted and ended up in the bin.

Mom had not allowed him to lick the melted cheese either, and he was hopping mad about it.

Fromage moaned:

>"My cheese, my wonderful cheese thrown in the bin!
>"Mom shouldn't have done that!!
>"I am going to starve to death tonight!!!
>"Mom will be sorry when she finds a skeleton tomorrow morning instead of her great kitty Fromage!!!!"

"A skeleton indeed! Fromage, it would take many moons to turn you into a SKELETON!" said Cara crossly.

"You were stinking up our cottage, and that just before Christmas too," ended Cara.

"What stink?" shouted Fromage as he glowered at her.

"The most glorious fragrance in the world – the aroma of French Cheese!

"Cara, you have no idea what you are talking about!!!"

The squabble simmered off as Cara stalked out angrily.

10 Days Before Christmas

Tuesday Morning:

The next day, Polo came over to our house.

"Guess who I met at the park early this morning?" yapped Polo.

Before we could respond, he answered the question himself.

Polo is, by nature, an excitable doggie with a tendency to go into a high-pitched yap whenever he became agitated.

Nevertheless, he had a heart of gold.

In my opinion, Polo was an OK pal.

Though now comfortably off, Polo had gone through some rough patches in life.

"You all remember Boss, don't you?" continued Polo.

What a question!!!

I felt a shudder run through my furry family.

Of course, we did!

In fact, we had been advised by both Monk and Polo to steer clear away from Boss.

To be honest, he frightened the daylights out of us.

Boss was a tough Rottweiler dog who lived down the street next to Polo's house.

Boss was big and strong and reputed to have a vicious streak.

He went with his master to the park every morning with his head held high.

He had a hoity-toity expression on his face with snooty airs towards any animal that was not at least as tall as him.

The only cat that he had any respect for was Monk. Monk could be menacing when it pleased him.

We had seen Boss walk by from the safety of our home. None of us dared to meet him face-to-face.

"I met him at the park this morning," said Polo.

"He actually came up to me and asked me how I was. He then whispered that he wished very much to meet the gang who solved the mystery of my Señora's lost diamond necklace."

The story of the diamond necklace had spread around like wild fire amongst the animal kingdom of Kensington.

We had become the talk of the town.

Terrance, in any case, had a glorious reputation due to having a great detective as his master and assisting him in solving many crimes. He was a hero and well respected by all the dogs, cats and other animals in the neighborhood and beyond.

I was pleased to note that my name as a good snoop was getting around too.

"I invited him over," said Polo.

"What?" I gasped. The hair on the back of my neck raised in horror despite myself.

We were going to have Boss amongst us?!

I saw Cara visibly shrink. Cara is timid by nature and tries to avoid unpleasant situations.

To be honest, I was not too thrilled about meeting Bully-Boy-Boss either. He gave me the shivers.

Just at that moment, Monk strolled in.

"What's going on? Why is everyone looking as if they have been hit with a bat?" he meowed.

Polo repeated his conversation with Boss to Monk.

"I cannot refuse any doggie in need, YOU understand don't you Monk?" barked Polo excitedly justifying his invitation to Boss.

There was a sudden scratching sound at our door.

"That must be Boss," said Polo.

Monk strolled to the door and opened it. Monk is clever that way. He is able to jump up and turn any door handle with ease.

It was Boss at the door.

He looked even more scary when one saw him close-up.

I went and stood next to Monk because this is my territory and more importantly because my nosiness got the better of me.

I needed to be at the forefront of every situation. I am the first to admit that I am a pretty NOSEY snoopy cat!

Boss stood there with a surprisingly meek look on his face.

"What can we do for you, Boss?" said Monk.

I was surprised at Boss's humble manner.

The Boss who stood before us was very different from the haughty bully we normally saw strutting down the street with his master Ned.

Boss looked worried and down in the dumps.

"May I please come in GRrrrrr?" He asked in a soft growl far removed from his usually loud sharp bark.

We looked at each other and I gave a nod to Monk.

"Come on in," said Monk. "What is the matter? are you sick?"

"No, it's more serious than that... GRrrrrr," Boss rasped.

More serious than being sick? Something grim must have happened.

"It looks as if I will be parted from Ned who is going to lose his home, GRrrrrr" Boss howled in a sad voice.

He went on to explain that Ned had lived in the house owned by old Mr. Finchley since he was a toddler. Mr. Finchley had been a crusty old bachelor and the owner of a well-known chocolate factory.

Ned's parents had been working as missionaries in Africa. Mr. Finchley being a close friend of his father, had invited Ned to live with him. Ned's parents had fallen ill in Africa and had moved to the other world in the blue skies.

Ned had continued to live with Mr. Finchley whom he called uncle.

Mr. Finchley has passed away a few weeks ago.

Ned had never been legally adopted by Mr. Finchley. Boss was not sure of the details as he had come to Ned as a puppy, when Ned was grown up. All he knew was that Ned had lived with Mr. Finchley since he was four years old.

Mr. Finchley had willed the house to Ned and told him about it when he fell ill. He had even shown him a legal paper, his last will, that said so.

Mr. Finchley had a nephew named Cyril who was of the same age as Ned. Cyril had been working with his uncle for some time and had eventually taken over his uncle's reputable chocolate factory when the old man became sick.

While Mr. Finchley had willed the valuable house to Ned, his nephew Cyril would take over the family business along with the other properties of even greater value than the house.

Ned, who had loved Mr. Finchley deeply, had been more worried about his sickness rather than owning his property and had not paid much attention to him when he spoke about his will.

Cyril had come to live with them ever since his uncle became sick and Ned had been fully occupied caring for old Mr. Finchley when he could no longer get up from his bed.

It now turned out that the will was missing and Cyril claimed that the house too belonged to him. He had asked Ned to move out of the house.

Cyril had given Ned a three-month's grace period to find a new place to live.

Ned, not being the smartest peg on the block, couldn't trace the will which was given to him by his uncle. He was in a miserable state at the thought of leaving the only home he had ever known.

Worst of all, Ned loved Boss and couldn't bear to be parted from him.

Hard to believe anyone loving Boss, but some humans had weird tastes, I thought to myself.

Cyril had told Ned that he would need Boss as a watchdog for the house and he would have to leave Boss behind when he moved out.

Boss was an EXCELLENT watchdog!

We all knew this since he didn't allow a cat, let alone a thief, to pass by without making a roaring din about it.

Boss looked woe-be-gone at the very thought of losing Ned.

We had heard from Polo that Ned was Boss's buddy and had looked after him since he came to the Finchley household. Ned groomed Boss daily and fed him nutritious stuff.

Ned's favorite pastime was keeping Boss in peak condition. They went for jogs to the park every morning.

"Cyril hates any type of exercise and prefers resting on his armchair eating away rather than jogging in the park with me, GRrrrr," growled Boss.

Boss counted on his toes reasons he detested Cyril:

"Cyril was a greedy fatso... GRrrr

"Cyril repeatedly belched loudly.... GRrrrr

"Cyril let off stink bombs all evening after eating like a pig... GRrrrrr

"Cyril was rude and nasty to Ned.... GRrrrrrr

"Most importantly: Cyril didn't love me as Ned did..... GRrrrrrrr"

Boss sighed!

"What a stinker! .... GRrrr

"Imagine being stuck with that nasty pig Cyril...... GRrrrr

"No more daily walks and running in the park...... GRrrrrr."

Boss hung his head really low and gave a long mournful groan.

"GGRrrrrRRrrrrrrrrrrr GGRrrrrrRRRRRRRRRR Rrrrrr!!!!!!!!!!!!!!!!!!!!!!"

It was strange seeing this pitiful side of Boss.

We had heard such scary stories about him that in our minds, Boss was someone that we kitties should avoid at all costs, for fear of our lives.

I decided to christen Cyril "The Stinky Porkster," there and then.

Nothing like a code name to add some pep to our adventure.

The others were thrilled by this new name.

Fromage went tumbling around the room shouting:

"Take this you Stinky Porkster! - Thump... whack!

"Thump...thump...whack...whack! - Take that you Stinky Porkster!"

Fromage, in his mind, was fighting a real live enemy and winning.

WINNING BIG-TIME, I may add.

We all knew that Fromage imagined himself to be a real live HERO.

But the end result was that he looked more comical than ever. He tended to look like a melting popsicle when he plopped down on the floor after one of his brave hero acts.

Boss grinned!

Marvelously, Fromage had managed to cheer-up Boss.

Who could not help but smile when Fromage acted as a hero?

He did look comical.

Despite my fear of Boss, I hated to see anyone down in the dumps.

I felt it was a shame for a proud doggie like Boss to look so sad, even though he had been a dreadful terror up to now.

I looked at Monk to see his reaction.

Polo looked at Monk with pleading eyes.

Polo the softy's heart had already melted.

He had forgiven Boss for his haughty behavior of the past.

Monk glanced at Polo and looked calculatingly at Boss.

He suddenly made up his mind and winked at me unknown to the others.

"Yep, we will help you, but on one condition Boss", rasped Monk.

"You must give me your word of honor that from this day onwards you will treat us cats, not only me, but ALL CATS with the utmost respect."

Boss gasped.

"GRrrrrrrrrrrrrrrrr!" went Boss in shock.

"What do you mean, Monk GRrrrr?" he barked.

"Just the cats in this compound, right GRrrrr." he woofed loudly eying Cara, Fromage and me.

"You don't expect me to be friends with all those cats trying to sneak in to my property? Surely not? GRrrrr?"

As you may have noticed by now, Boss had a habit of ending all his conversations with a "GRrrrr."

Quite alarming, if you didn't know him.

Monk stood firm.

"No, Boss! I mean every single cat in the world and of course Charlotte," he said pointing at Charlotte peering out from the safety of her little cage.

Boss gave a glance at Charlotte and his arrogance surfaced once again.

"When have I been interested in such little creatures? GRrrrrr?" he snarled.

"Who or what is that anyway? GRrrrrr?" Boss added baring his long sharp teeth.

I saw looks of annoyance from both Polo and Fromage.

What cheek asking for our help and insulting our friend! How dare he speak of Charlotte in such a manner?

As for Charlotte, she had stopped in her tracks when she heard Boss speak about her.

She turned her back on him in scorn, her nose quivering in rage.

I noted her thought process:

"Ugly monster!

"Gross mutt!

"I will creep into his ear and dance in his brain."

Boss is not unintelligent. He immediately realized he had made the biggest blunder of his life and quickly retracted.

"I am sorry. GRrrrrr," he said, his front paws covering his nose

"Of course! I include Charlotte in the group that I will protect from this day onwards. GRrrrrr.

"Not only will I treat ALL cats with respect, but also Charlotte, who I have heard, is the cleverest hamster in Kensington. GRrrrrr."

Flattery will get you everywhere!

Everyone's ruffled fur settled down, including that of Charlotte's.

Charlotte beamed at him in approval.

Quick turnaround, I noted.

We agreed that we would all go over to Boss's house later that evening to do some real detective work.

We also decided that Polo would not accompany us.

Monk, Fromage and I would have to enter Boss's compound by leaping from trees and roofs, and Polo would not be able to manage that being a doggie.

Polo looked disappointed, but even he could see the wisdom of this plan and reluctantly agreed on the condition that we would tell him all on our return.

Cara preferred to cuddle up to Mom instead of roaming the night climbing trees. So, it was agreed that she would not join us either.

Tuesday Afternoon:

Just for a test run, Monk asked Fromage and me to come with him while it was daylight to take a look at Boss's house from the safety of the wall between Boss's and Polo's house.

While I was determined to help out Boss, I could not help being uneasy about this case.

Could we really help Boss and Ned keep their house?

I had no idea where to start. I would have to piggyback on Monk for this case.

My earlier intention to resolve the next mystery by myself was slowly fading away.

We all went over to Polo's house through the hole in the hedge between our houses.

While Polo, Charlotte and Cara stayed in Polo's garden, Monk, Fromage and I climbed on to the wall after climbing up a tree.

It was not an easy climb. We struggled through, sat on the wall and observed Boss's house and garden.

The house was large with a two-car garage and an even larger garden.

In the garage, a tiny old car was sitting next to a shiny large car.

Boss appeared below the wall and looked up at us.

"I will meet you right here tonight. GRrrrrr" he rasped.

"The bedrooms are on the other side of the house. This is the back garden. The small car belongs to Ned and the fancy car belongs to the Stinky Porkster. GRrrrrr."

Not too difficult a jump down, I thought, even though the wall was quite high. I hoped it wasn't too high for Fromage. He had struggled a bit and fallen down twice when we had climbed the tree. Fortunately, he had landed on a soft bush.

Despite the falls, I wouldn't dream of asking Fromage to stay behind. He loves any type of adventure and would create a huge hullabaloo if he couldn't be in it.

In any case, he would certainly refuse.

Tuesday Night:

It was 11 p.m.

Fromage and I slipped out of our cottage.

Monk was waiting for us on the back porch of his house.

We followed Monk to Boss's house leaping over fences and crawling under shrubs.

When it came to climbing up a large tree to land on Boss's high wall, I nudged Fromage ahead of me. I was aware that our Fromage is a bit clumsy.

"Slow and steady, sink your claws into the branch at each step. Don't look down; just keep your eyes on Monk," I whispered in Fromage's ears.

Fromage cautiously clambered up the tree.

We finally arrived on Boss's high wall, without further mishap. The top of the wall was wide and gave us sufficient space to comfortably settle down.

I was glad that Fromage had managed the climb with no problems.

Fromage gave me his cheeky grin!

"Remember the times we used to visit Charlotte over the rooftops of Paris, Sis?"

How could I forget?

"Yes Fromage. Remember watching the iron lady—Eiffel dancing in her sparkling gown?" I said.

Boss was indeed a great watchdog. His senses were very sharp. No sooner than we settled on his wall, he came charging through the dog flap of his back door.

Only this time, he did not make a sound—no barking at all. He came at us like a bullet and settled down close below us.

"Can you jump down easily? GRrrrrr?" he asked.

I looked down. It was a really high wall. I could manage it and so could Monk, but I was thinking about Fromage.

Boss's sharp eyes seemed to have caught my uncertainty in the pale light of the moon.

"Not to worry. GRrrrr" he rasped.

"Just follow me. GRrrrr."

Turning around quickly, he ran swiftly along the wall to a point where there was a clump of shrubs, growing from the ground all the way up to the top of the wall. Clutching onto the shrub, we slipped down easily.

It was a breeze even for clumsy Fromage.

"Thank you all for coming. GRrrrr" said Boss gratefully.

"No worries, Boss," I replied.

"Let's go. GRrrrr," said Boss.

He stopped at a window and we stood on tiptoe to look in. We saw a large comfortable room where a podgy man was seated puffing on a pipe with a HUGE plate of sweets clutched in his ham like heavy fist.

Boss looked at him with an anxious expression.

"That's the Stinky Porkster.... GRrrrrr" he said.

"Ned used to sit on that same chair every evening. But since he couldn't tolerate the smoke of the cigar, he has retreated to the kitchen. GRrrrrr."

Boss moved to the next large window where we saw Ned sitting at the kitchen table. He was looking into his cup of cocoa miserably.

"I see that Ned does not have his usual happy-go-lucky face," said Monk.

"That's right. GRrrrrr" replied Boss.

"I have a great deal of trouble getting him to go on our usual run in the mornings. GRrrrrr.

"I believe, it is only because of me that he makes the effort. GRrrrr.

"He understands the importance of keeping a dog like me in tip-top physical condition. GRrrrr."

I secretly studied Boss's physique.

I would give him that—Boss was in superb condition. His lean muscles rippled when he moved and his black coat was shiny with clearly defined tan markings.

Boss's kitchen was very spacious. We could see a large furnace well-lit with crackling wood and a huge basket which we thought was for Boss to lie close to the fire.

"Tell us something about Ned and your life," said Monk.

"Not much to say. GRrrrr." Boss began.

"Ned spends a lot of the time caring for me. Daily brushings, jogs in the park and preparing my food from scratch. He loves cooking and used to take care of his uncle, very carefully preparing delicious soups. GRrrrr.

"Unfortunately, the old man could not eat towards the latter part of his life. Ned was very attached to old Mr. Finchley. GRrrrrr.

"We have a man named Rolf who lives in and takes care of the house and garden, but it is his day off. He should be back soon. GRrrrrr.

"Rolf is one tough, ugly guy, but I generally ignore him as he doesn't like dogs and considers me just a watch dog. GRrrrrr.

"Another reason why I detest Rolf is because he is very close to the Stinky Porkster. GRrrrrr."

"What about the will that you spoke about?" said Monk.

"Were you there when the old man gave it to Ned?"

"I believe so. GRrrrrr" said Boss, screwing up his nose and brow, trying to think back.

"Unfortunately, I have a very short memory span. GRrrrrr.

"But I always followed Ned around the house and when he used to take Old Mr. Finchley his meals, I accompanied him carrying his serviette. GRrrrrr.

"I must have been there for sure. GRrrrrr."

"Try to give it some thought, Boss," said Monk.

"If you can remember that day, it would give us a clue in tracing the will."

Boss shook his head and then shook it again hard.

I looked at him in alarm.

I thought his head would fly off.

"I just don't seem to remember. Sorry Monk. GRrrrrr," said Boss, looking rather flustered.

I remembered most things by allowing my mind to wander and ponder over things. I thought that perhaps Boss would succeed if he tried to do this as well.

"Don't worry about it now," I told him. "Give it some thought later on."

Just then the lights in the living room were switched off and we saw the Stinky Porkster climb the stairs to go to his room.

In a little while, we saw Ned get up from the chair at the kitchen dining-table and with his cocoa still in his hand, take the back stairs up to his bedroom.

Monk suddenly had an idea.

"Boss, can you take us to the room that old Mr. Finchley occupied? Perhaps by relating what happened that day, you may remember more details," said Monk.

We went to the back door and entered Boss's house through the large dog flap.

The house somewhat resembled the house that was occupied by the Señora and Polo. A large house with spacious rooms and plenty of space.

Old Mr. Finchley's room was downstairs. He had moved into the library when he had fallen ill and it was too difficult for him to climb the stairs.

There were shelves of books still lining the entire room. A large bed had also been placed in the middle of the room.

The room was empty with the bed neatly made. All of old Mr. Finchley's things had been boxed and given away to charity.

We sat on the carpet and Monk asked Boss to think back to that day and describe what he remembered.

Boss closed his eyes and started speaking slowly.

"I remember old Mr. Finchley sitting on the bed propped up by a great number of pillows. It was summer time and Ned had left the window open so that Mr. Finchley could hear the birds singing in the trees outside. It was one of Mr. Finchley's better days and though weak, he was smiling. GRrrrrr.

"I remember now. GRrrrrr," continued Boss.

"The Stinky Porkster had come to see Mr. Finchley that day. They were talking about the chocolate factory when Ned came in with Mr. Finchley's supper. I trailed behind him carrying his serviette. GRrrrrr.

"Mr. Finchley liked me bringing his serviette to him. He took it, patted me on the head, called me a 'good doggie' and asked me to look after the house. GRrrrrr.

"After Ned set down the tray, Mr. Finchley handed over the will to him and said that the house was left to Ned and the factory to Cyril.

"Mr. Finchley added that he was doing this now since he did not know as to how many more days he had to live. GRrrrrr.

"At that moment, I recall Ned breaking down and kneeling by Mr. Finchley's bed and burying his head on his lap. Ned was very upset. After some time, Ned left the room and I left with him. That is all I can remember GRrrrrr.

"Is that good enough, Monk GRrrrrr?" he asked eagerly.

"Not bad at all old chap," said Monk. "You did well enough."

Monk asked Boss to stay with Fromage downstairs while he and I did a quick inspection of the rooms upstairs.

The upstairs had two sections. One part seemed to be for Ned. The other, formerly occupied by old Mr. Finchley, had been taken over by The Stinky Porkster.

None of the doors were firmly shut and Monk and I were able to push them open and check the rooms. Both the Stinky Porkster and Ned seemed to be fast asleep. Both were snoring in different tones.

"SNOOOOOOOOOOORE!"
Went the Stinky Porkster loudly.

"ZZZZZZZZZZZZZZZZ!
Went Ned in a softer tone.

Both rooms had large windows overlooking the garden. There were lots of trees outside which would give easy access to anyone trying to enter the house through them.

The Porkster and Ned seemed to like fresh air because all the windows had been left open with the curtains flapping lightly in the wind. Both rooms had their own small fireplaces which were crackling with burning wood.

However, I doubted any thief would be able to sneak into the house, since Boss was circling around it at all times. I guess that is why the windows were open. The household was secure with Boss guarding it.

We went downstairs, collected Fromage and said goodnight to Boss. We asked him to keep thinking back and if he remembered anything else, to let Polo know when he met him in the park the next morning.

Promising to come back soon, Monk returned to his house. Fromage and I returned to ours.

9 Days Before Christmas

Wednesday Morning:

My team and I had several pow-wows in Monk's library, wondering as to what could have happened to old Mr. Finchley's LAST WILL.

We all came to the conclusion that it was obvious that the Stinky Porkster had something to do with it.

Just by looking at him, I had been deeply suspicious of the Stinky Porkster. The fact that he was in the room with old Mr. Finchley the day Boss saw the will for the last time was a deciding factor.

To be fair, Monk and I decided to set out the case before the rest of the group.

Monk started off by asking everyone to say who they thought had taken the document.

We sat in a circle and passed around blank pieces of paper. Each of us had to write the name of who they thought was guilty before putting it in the center of the circle.

A SECRET BALLOT --- WOW!!!

After 10 minutes, we opened the papers and found the same answer written on each of them.

We all suspected the Stinky Porkster!

He was the only one who had a motive and the ability to pinch the will.

Hah! Hah!

Not such a difficult case to crack after all, I thought.

Monk looked at us with a pleased expression and said, "Good work team."

"Are we real detectives now?" asked Polo.

"We are indeed," said Monk. "If Terrance had been here, he would have given all of you all gold stars."

Polo looked very pleased at this compliment as he was a great admirer of Terrance and very proud to be his neighbor and friend.

"Shall we give ourselves a name?" Polo asked. "After all, this is the second case we are working on together."

"Once our reputation spreads, we are surely going to solve other cases. You know, the other dogs I meet in the park always ask me how we solved the case of Señora's missing diamond necklace," smirked Polo.

"Why not?" said Monk with a smile.

"Cat Detectives of Kensington," meowed Cara softly.

"But I am not a cat," moaned Polo. "And neither is Terrance."

"Oops!" said Cara.

"What about ... Inca & Company?" said Fromage.

"Fromage, that would not be fair," I said, though actually, I was as pleased as punch.

"Why should Monk and Polo, or even Terrance, accept my name to head our detective agency?"

Fromage just looked at me with his saucer eyes. Fromage is one loyal bro!

Monk jumped in before Fromage could respond.

"A very fine name," he said. "How about it Polo? Do you agree?"

Polo gave a wide grin, his little pink tongue hanging out, as he panted.

"Of course! Inca is my heroine. You know she saved Charlotte when she was hurt on top of your roof last summer. Our detective agency could not have a better name."

"Hip, hip, hooray," shouted Cara, giving me a lick.

"Inca & Company is the name of our new detective agency."

I was bursting with pride but reminded myself to be casual and not show my true feelings. I looked at my team of detectives.

"I promise you that I will make you proud for having named the agency after me," was all I allowed myself to say, trying to be modest.

What I actually wanted to do was dance the jig in delight with my signature stern face!

8 Days Before Christmas

Thursday Morning:

Yesterday was a special day, I scribbled in my Diary.

Imagine a detective agency named after me!

I had to live up to my name now, which was both flattering and a huge responsibility. At the same time, I was determined to make our new detective agency a huge success.

If we cracked this case, our reputation would be established. All the doggies who met daily at the park would know of us and spread the news. The doggies who walked or who were walked in Kensington Park were a gossipy lot.

No doubt about it. Soon we would have a popular detective agency. Since my name was involved, it was up to me to cement the reputation of the company by solving this mystery.

With regard to this case, the decision had been made. We were all convinced that the Stinky Porkster had stolen the will, the legal paper, handing over the house to Ned.

Other questions arose:

- ❖ "Where had he hidden it?"
- ❖ "Could he have already destroyed the will?"
- ❖ "Could he have taken it with him to his office and hidden it there?"
- ❖ "Even if it was in his room, how could we find it?"

I couldn't get this case out of my head.

Was there a possibility for me to solve it by myself?

I decided to go over and speak to Boss. I knew that the Stinky Porkster went to work, but what about Ned? Ned did not go to work. He was a computer geek and he worked from home. But with Boss's help, maybe I could do more snooping around without Ned noticing that I was there.

I crept over the ceilings, walls, and up the trees of our neighbors, and soon arrived on Boss's wall.

Everything was quiet. I could see from my position on the wall that Ned was in his room, his head down, working on his computer.

As expected, Boss came dashing out of the house. He had sensed an intruder – a cat on his premises.

He did not bark. He was being faithful to his promise to Monk and intelligent enough to realize that I had not paid him a visit solely to enjoy his company.

"Howdy Boss," I said. Can we have a chat?"

"Sure. GRrrrr," he said.

"Come along to the kitchen. I am by myself. Ned will not come down until lunchtime. Even if he does, he has no objections to cats. Actually, he rather likes Monk. He always tries to stop and pet him if we meet him on the way to the park, GRrrrr."

I ran to the shrub at the far end, slipped down the branches to the ground and followed Boss into the kitchen.

We sat on his huge cot. I told him about what we had discussed last night and the conclusion we had reached.

Boss looked at me shrewdly.

"This is what I suspected as well GRrrrr," he said.

"Ned thinks the same. He told me so. But he is too timid to challenge The Stinky Porkster. I believe he feels guilty that old Mr. Finchley decided to leave the house to him, an outsider, instead of to his flesh and blood, the Stinky Porkster. GRrrrr.

"However, he never expected the Stinky Porkster to ask him to leave the house. GRrrrrr.

"Ned is a simpleton. He thought that the Stinky Porkster and he could continue to share the house and live together like a family since neither of them had any family left. GRrrrrr" Boss concluded.

"Boss," I said. "I want to go into Stinky Porkster's room and search it."

"The Stinky Porkster is always careful to lock his door before he leaves. GRrrrrr." said Boss.

"He never did this before but since of late he is very careful to lock his door. As if Ned or I would want to go into the Stinker's room anyway. GRrrrrr.

"You may have to wait until he comes back home. GRrrrrr."

"Let's go outside," I said.

I remembered the large tree just next to Stinky Porkster's room that Monk and I had noticed when we last took a look around upstairs.

I looked thoughtfully at the windows. Although Boss could not get up to the room that way, I could.

One of my favorite pastimes is balancing on narrow ledges and leaping onto surfaces out of the reach of others.

The branches leaning towards the Stinky Porkster's bedroom looked sturdy enough to withstand my weight.

I made a decision.

Time was running out and I could not get the thought of investigating the Stinky Porkster's room out of my head.

I realized that this was my great chance to play the role of a great snoop and do something thrilling.

My inquisitiveness got the better of me.

I clambered up the tree like an old pro with Boss looking on with his eyes nearly popping out of his head. I got the feeling he was impressed.

Just for his benefit, I airily leaped from one branch to another which brought me closer to the window.

Soon I was looking into the Stinky Porkster's bedroom. I waved to Boss, who was looking at me with his tongue hanging out, and leaped without difficulty from the branch right onto the Porkster's bed.

Good-EEE! A pretty soft landing.

"Piece of cake!" I thought to myself smugly.

I took a quick look around.

Everything seemed to be in place: A large bed, a wardrobe, an armchair, a bookshelf with green leather-bound books all of the same size and two writing tables.

I climbed onto one desk and delicately pushed the papers around, trying to peek at every one of them.

Despite my being careful, no way would the Stinky Porkster not notice that someone had been browsing through his papers.

"Nothing ventured, nothing gained," I murmured to myself, and decided to do a thorough job of it.

I jumped into his clothes cupboard.

❖ Nope, nothing there other than his clothes.

I carefully went through another writing table near his bed.

❖ Nope, nothing there either, other than some unpaid bills.

I poked my head into his shoe cupboard.

❖ Nope, nothing there but shoes, slippers and shoe polish.

I looked under his bed.

❖ Nope, nothing there.

I looked between the sheets.

❖ Nope, nothing there.

I searched high and low but could not find the will.

❖ Nope! Nothing! Nada!

I looked around the room. Every single place had been checked.

I wondered why the Stinky Porkster took so much trouble to close the door and lock it so carefully. There was nothing of value in this room other than for some suits and shoes, expensive and very well used. No value for any thief to steal.

"Who would want those?" I wondered.

I sat on the bed, deep in thought, wondering what I should do next.

I decided to stay in the room, hiding until the Stinky Porkster got back.

I leaped out of the window and quickly went down to let Boss know of my decision.

While I was examining the Stinky Porkster's room the sky had turned gray. It looked as if it was about to start raining.

I shuddered.

If there is one thing that I hated – it was getting wet.

UGH!!

I quickly rattled off what I had planned to Boss.

Boss looked surprised at my decision.

"Are you sure, Inca? GRrrrrr," he asked.

"I wouldn't want you to get into difficulties. GRrrrrr. Monk and your family may not be pleased that you are by yourself in a locked room. Why don't you go get Monk to help you? GRrrrrr."

"It's too late now?" I meowed back quickly and reassuringly.

"After all, we are detectives and this is what we usually do."

More importantly, I did not want him to guess that I wanted to solve this case by myself.

To be honest, I wanted to take all the glory for myself.

Before he could protest, I dashed up the tree, jumped back into the room and looked for a good place to hide.

Under the bed was the best place, I decided, and curled myself into a ball to keep warm.

Thursday Afternoon:

I woke up with a start to the sound of a key turning in the lock.

A light was snapped on and the Stinky Porkster's fat body entered the room letting out stink bombs as he plodded into the room.

Looking at him closely, I had to agree with Boss.

Not a very pleasant sight, was Boss's Porkster. NOT a pleasant smell either.

I hadn't observed the Stinky Porkster this close before:

- ❖ The Stinky Porkster was perfectly round.
- ❖ His face was as round as was his body.
- ❖ He had a smug expression on his face, as if bullying was his favorite pastime.

I realized that Ned would never stand a chance with this great big bully.

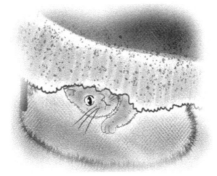

He had a very long nose and his eyes made him look like the very devil himself.

Boss had warned me about this. Even so, I felt a shiver run down my spine looking at his demonic eyes.

He gave a startled groan when he saw his messy papers and stomped out of the room.

"Boss! Ned! Who went into my room?" bellowed the Stinky Porkster.

Boy! Did he have a loud harsh voice to go with his round head, round face and even rounder body!

It was clear to me that the Stinky Porkster suspected Ned.

A confused Ned came into my view with Boss sheepishly slinking in behind him.

"No one," said Ned. "I've been at home the whole day and Boss never made a sound. The door was locked after all."

The Stinky Porkster glared at Ned.

He had known Ned for a long time and realized that Ned would never think of doing such a thing.

In his opinion, Ned was a simpleton, a wishy-washy do-gooder with the courage of a dish cloth.

"Someone came in this way. I am sure of it. My things are messed up!" said the Stinky Porkster and rushed to the window.

"It must be Rolf cleaning after you," said Ned mildly.

Ned shook his head and left the room with Boss.

The Stinky Porkster slammed the door and locked it. After he did this, he looked around and went to the bookshelf.

I watched him carefully, not daring to breathe. Would he search under the bed?

Naaah!

The Stinky Porkster didn't look the kind of fatso who would bother to go down on his chubby knees and peer under the bed.

It looked as if I would be safe as long as I didn't make a sound.

He carefully opened a large green book from the shelf and looked inside. He removed a folded paper, sighed with relief, carefully put it back and placed the book on the shelf again.

He continued to put his belongings in order. He then took a quick look around the room, went out and relocked the door behind him.

I sat pondering and wondering why the Stinky Porkster did not destroy the will. Surely, that would have been the easiest thing to do? I wished I could get into his mind to read what was going on in it!

Could it be that he still loved his uncle and could not bring himself to destroy the will?

No time to ponder, I thought.

What was I to do?

A thought sprang to my mind.

Should I climb the shelf and pull the book down?

Could I do it without making much noise so that the Stinky Porkster would not rush back into the room and catch me in the act?

I needed some help. I decided to leave the room through the window and discuss this with Boss.

On the ground, Boss was waiting for me. He sighed with relief when he saw me. I told him what had happened.

"What a relief that he didn't find you hiding under the bed. I've been so worried about you. GRrrrrr."

"The Stinky Porkster would never bend down to check under it. Too much exercise for his fat body," I said with a sneer.

I looked at him triumphantly.

"I have discovered where the Stinky Porkster has hidden the will.

"We now need to decide how we can get it out of the room. I could do this by myself, but I need your help.

"I am worried that when I pull the book down from the shelf, the noise would bring the Stinky Porkster running back upstairs.

"How do we get the Stinky Porkster out of the house? If he leaves the house for at least 10 minutes, it would give me enough time to get at the document," I concluded.

Boss wrinkled his nose, deep in thought and said --

"There is only one thing that the Stinky Porkster loves more than himself. That is his car. He cleans it himself every Sunday and lavishes attention on it as if it were a newborn baby. If he thought anything would happen to it, he would be out of the house in a jiffy. GRrrrrr."

Boss thought for a minute.

"Inca, GRrrrrr" he said.

"Climb back into his room. I am going to create a commotion near his car. GRrrrrr.

"Listen for my bark. GRrrrrr."

"Up I go," I said and gave Boss an airy wave.

In a few minutes, I returned to the room and hid under the bed.

After some time, I heard Boss's ferocious bark from the side of the house where the Stinky Porkster's much loved car was parked.

I then heard the Stinky Porkster's loud voice and heard him as he crashed out of the house and banged the side door.

I did not hesitate.

I immediately jumped on the shelf and pulled at the large book that I had seen the Stinky Porkster examining.

Horror of horrors!!

I could not make the book budge. It was tightly packed between the other books.

I desperately pulled, knowing that the Stinky Porkster could walk back into the room at any moment.

What would he do if he found a strange cat in his room?

I could probably dart out of the window having noticed how unfit the Stinky Porkster was.

But the whole purpose would be lost as he surely would take the paper and disappear out of the house or destroy it.

Our one and only chance would be lost forever.

Should I leave the room now and come back with Monk who was much stronger?

Hmmm.... that would take the case right out of my own hands.

I am ashamed to admit that I really wished to crack this case by myself.

After all the team had named our Detective Agency after me.

I couldn't let the side down.

The sheer desperation of the situation made me use all my strength.

I latched my nails onto the binder of the book.

I pulled with all my might.

THUD!

The book crashed to the ground with a THUMP.

The folded paper floated down and rested on the floor.

PHEW!!!

What a relief!!!

I bent down to take a look at the paper.

Yep, it was the WILL.

Suddenly!

CRASH!!!

The door burst open and the Stinky Porkster stood at the door...

My heart stood still!

I looked at the Stinky Porkster in horror!

The sight of me bending over the will had turned him into a mad demon.

THIEF! THIEF!

He yelled!

His face had turned purple. He looked not only like a mad demon but a mad demon about to have a fit.

I shuddered, the fur on my neck standing on end.

Cyril the Porkster had turned into a purple monster and a demon combined in one horrid fat body.

For a second, I couldn't move as I was terrified! I stood glued to the floor!

All my bravado disappeared in a jiffy.

I pulled myself out of my state of terror.

It's 'now or never' I thought to myself desperately.

I had to make a run for it.

I grabbed the paper in my mouth and leaped to the window.

But I had not anticipated the nasty rain.

The blast of stormy rain gave me a rude shock.

I nearly let out a loud meow in my surprise at the cold wet rain.

Just in time, I remembered the valuable paper I carried and clamped it tighter in my mouth.

My hesitation at the window had given the Stinky Porkster time to move.

I heard the Stinky Porkster's loud voice utter a snarl and his hot stinky breath pour over me.

"Got you" he said as his fat fist reached out and grabbed me.

The Stinky Porkster yanked me to the ground and held me down.

I struggled with all my might but I couldn't wriggle free.

My heart beat wildly:

Bang! Boom! Bang!

What a disaster!!!

What would he do?

* ❖ Would this be the end of my wonderful short life?

- ❖ Would he crush me under his big fat feet??
- ❖ Would he rip my head off???
- ❖ Would he chew me up like a chocolate????
- ❖ Would he swallow me whole like a marshmallow????
- ❖ Would I end up turning into a snack for this ugly purple monster??????

How did I get myself into this pickle?

Just then Boss came charging into the room barking very, very loudly.

"WOOF! WOOF! WOOF!

The Stinky Porkster was distracted by Boss's hurried and noisy dash into the room.

This made him lose his grip and I managed to wriggle out of his grasp.

I guess he expected Boss to catch me and rip me to pieces.

The Stinky Porkster was well aware of Boss's reputation for destroying kitties.

"Catch her Boss!"

Yelled the Stinky Porkster, making the glass windows rattle at the loud roar of his voice.

Boss winked at me whilst snarling. Taking that as a sign of encouragement, I leaped out of the window using all my strength.

My famous talent for leaping came into good use.

I landed on the tree and clutched on to the branch for dear life.

The rain had turned the branches wet and slippery. My paws were damp and I felt myself sliding down the trunk.

I dug my claws deeper into the slippery trunk and continued to climb down in spite of being worried that I would slip and fall.

I slithered to the ground and hid under a shrub.

I stayed as still as I could, panting with the force of my descent.

I was safe for the moment but I was shivering from the cold.

The will, a single paper, was not heavy. Thankfully, it was folded and I could hold it firmly in my mouth.

Another worry - I was more nervous that the paper would turn into a soggy mess due to the water from the rain.

I heard a commotion in the background and a loud voice shouting,

"Boss, after that cat!"

I forced myself to move from the safety of the shrub that protected me from the rain and raced for the wall.

I felt Boss's large paws coming after me, but rather slowly.

I guessed Boss was pretending to come after me but was actually running at a slower pace to give me a chance to escape.

Good old Boss!

Without thinking twice, I raced to the shrubbery by the wall and climbed it, forgetting the cold and my shivering body.

I raced back home.

Thursday Evening:

I was ever so happy to be back in our warm and cozy cottage.

I put down the document on our dining table where Mom would surely not miss seeing it.

I sat down panting.

I excitedly blabbed the story out to Cara who looked at me with awe.

"Inca, you are so brave," she said.

"Cara, quick run and go fetch Monk," I said. "I don't wish to leave this paper alone for one minute."

While waiting for Monk, I carefully opened the folded paper. Despite the dampness the writing was clear.

Here was the will, signed in the shaky but legible writing of old Mr. Finchley, gifting his house to Ned!!

It was countersigned with two other signatures and stamped.

I had done it!

I had achieved my dream of solving the case by myself.

I had become a detective par excellence!

"Well done!" said Monk as he padded in with Polo and Cara.

"The important thing is to tell Mom that she should protect this paper and call Ned pronto," I said through chattering teeth.

Despite my shivers, I couldn't help but be proud.

But I restrained myself from bragging.

In any case, my chattering teeth prevented me from doing so.

"I wish Solo was here," said Monk.

He was silent for a minute and then said:

"Inca can you get Mom to call Inspector Reid? He will know what to do about this. Yes, he will be a match for the Stinky Porkster."

Monk was correct.

No way did I want Mom to deal with someone like the Stinky Porkster alone.

"You are right, Monk," I said.

"I will do so as soon as she comes in from the store with Fromage. In the meantime, Cara and I will guard the will and see that it doesn't get in harm's way.

"Without this precious paper, Ned would be on the streets and Boss would be left to live with the Stinky Porkster.

"We cannot allow that. Despite how Boss has behaved in the past, he was now our client, and we must do our best for him."

"I think Boss has learnt his lesson," said Polo.

"He feels sorry for his past behavior and has nothing but admiration for you. I know he will keep to his promise. I am sure he will no longer bother kitties. No fear of that. Boss has his faults, but he is a doggie who keeps to his word."

"He was a great help in me getting away from the Stinky Porkster," I said in agreement.

No sooner had I uttered these words that we saw a strange ugly face looking in through the window.

Narrow slits for eyes, short stubble on his head, with a really ugly mug! He was staring at us with a menacing sneer on his face.

"Who is that?" I yowled nearly falling off the table.

"It's Rolf!" yapped Polo in excitement and fear as he recognized the nasty face peering at us.

The Stinky Porkster seemed to have sent Rolf after us instead of coming himself.

We looked at each other in alarm.

Where were our friendly humans when we needed them?

I began to have second thoughts about this whole adventure.

As much as I loved detective work, I didn't wish any of my furry family or friends to get hurt.

Rolf looked like a NASTY piece of work.

"Quick, quick, let's hide the will before he gets in," yelled Monk.

We heard him at the door fiddling with the lock.

Luckily the door was locked!

"He will be able to open the door with a false key. I have seen this done many times before by Solo and Hobbs," yowled Monk.

"Let's move it."

"HURRY! HURRY!

"I will take the will and go out through the window," shouted Monk.

"Hold on Monk!" I yelled.

"He will only come after you. He looks like a tough and fit guy. I know what to do, trust me.

"You just try to distract him."

While the door burst open, my friends charged at Rolf courageously, even my timid sis Cara.

I grabbed the will in my mouth and headed off to the attic, closely followed by Charlotte.

Charlotte had guessed what I had in mind.

We were heading to a place that Rolf would never be able to get to. Our playing field – the attic.

The attic was Charlotte's home and the spot we played our favorite game - Gangsters Verses Cops.

Our home was a proper cottage. There was an attic just below the thatched roof.

This space was awkwardly shaped and a human would find it difficult to walk upright in it.

Mom had reserved the attic as a playpen for her four-footed furry family.

As we left, I saw Monk landing on Rolf's shoulder digging his sharp claws into him.

No light weight was our pal Monk, I can assure you.

Rolf let out a shrill yell of surprise as Polo nipped his ankles with his sharp teeth and Cara hissed at him with all her might.

Looking at Rolf, I knew they couldn't stop him. But it did give Charlotte and me time to run up to the attic.

Charlotte gave a frightened squeak when we saw Rolf's angry face looming behind us with our team behind him.

Monk, noticing that I was a few feet from the landing to the attic, launched himself once again onto Rolf's back.

Rolf lost his step and went crashing down the stairs with this sudden weight on him.

I saw Monk had landed safely on his feet, as we kitties always do.

He jumped on Rolf once again.

With another burst of energy, I raced into the attic with Charlotte scurrying behind me.

"Over here," panted Charlotte and led me to a far corner where she had made a comfy nest.

She took the will in her teeny paws and pushed it deep inside.

Only she could enter this tiny space. Not even we could enter her private space as it was so small.

I was fairly sure that Rolf would not be able to get inside the attic.

Even if he crawled on his belly, he would not be able to reach into Charlotte's nest.

"Stay hidden with the paper, Charlotte," I said as we saw Rolf trying to squeeze himself into the attic.

I went forward, hissing angrily, though my heart was pounding with fear.

Rolf looked a nasty sullen character and I did not look forward to battling with him.

One thing though, he had a nasal voice which made his curses seem silly.

But his voice was the only thing silly about him.

In every other way, he was a huge, ugly, revolting man.

Rolf tried to crawl further into the room. His nasty, stinky breath made us want to puke.

UGH!!!

Just then we heard the sound of Mom's bicycle coming up the drive.

I sighed with relief.

For sure, Rolf did not want to get caught inside Mom's house, uninvited.

Muttering a low curse in his silly voice, Rolf crawled back out and ran down the stairs.

He leaped out of the window as Mom's key turned in the lock.

We collapsed in relief.

Rolf's role in the mystery soon became evident.

He was the Stinky Porkster's henchman.

He had planned to get a big fat bribe once the house became the Stinky Porkster's.

I recovered the paper from Charlotte and sped down the stairs.

Mom came in with Fromage. She wheeled her bicycle under the protection of the porch and Fromage jumped down from the basket that he rides in.

Monk and Polo left me to deal with Mom and quickly ran out through the back-door cat flap.

When Mom and Fromage came in, Cara and I were sitting solemnly in front of the paper on the dining table.

"Hello My little poppets! Why the long faces?" said Mom.

"Why aren't you running to greet me?

"What's going on?" added Mom when she noticed us crouching over the will.

Leaving Cara to explain to Fromage about what had happened, I jumped into Mom's arms.

I put my forepaws on her shoulders and looked deep into her eyes.

I started passing my thoughts t[...]
waves, explaining the need to ca[...]
Reid and hand over the will urgent[...]
save Ned from losing his house.

My telepathic powers were as strong [...]

Mom of course understood. She pic[...]
the will and read it without saying a wor[...]

"How you managed to get a hold of this w[...]
a wonder. I need to call Inspector Reid ri[...]
away" she said.

Mom knew Ned. They often met while jogging
in the park. Ned had told her about him having
to leave his home.

Mom lifted the phone and called Inspector
Reid. She explained excitedly about what was
going on. Inspector Reid promised to come
immediately.

Between you and me, I believed Inspector Reid
had a crush on Mom.

I'd noticed how he hung on every word she
said and simpered like an idiot whenever she
was around.

True to his word, Inspector Reid knocked on our door soon after.

He looked over our cozy sitting room. He eagerly accepted Mom's offer of hot chocolate which he sipped while listening to Mom.

Inspector Reid, like his friend Solo, was tall and lanky but with sandy brown hair unlike Solo's mop of black hair.

Monk claimed that Inspector Reid was a decent bloke even though he rarely smiled. However, Monk had to admit that after the Inspector met my family, particularly Mom, he was a changed person.

"You did very well calling me, Missy," he said and blushed when Mom expressed her thanks for him coming so quickly.

He studied the will carefully.

"Somehow, I suspect your kitties had something to do with this will," he said as he looked at the three of us.

We blinked at him, and then ignored him, each of us busy in our own way.

Fromage settled down before the fire.

Cara settled down on Mom's lap, glowering at the good Inspector.

I settled behind Mom's head, sniffing her fresh scented hair. She could then lean back and give me a quick stroke when she felt my breath on her neck.

Inspector Reid reluctantly got to his feet and held Mom's hands while saying his goodbyes.

"Is he ever going to let go of her hands?" muttered Cara crossly.

Cara is possessive of Mom.

"Come on Cara," I said. "He's just being friendly. He's is helping us after all."

In response, Cara scowled some more at Inspector Reid.

The good inspector had no idea about Cara's possessive jealousy. He promised Mom that he would deal with the will.

He had heard rumors of the Stinky Porkster asking Ned to leave his home. He assured Mom that he would make sure that Ned became the lawful owner of the house.

It would be the Stinky Porkster who would have to leave the house unless Ned agreed to let him stay on.

Inspector Reid couldn't understand why the Stinky Porkster wanted Ned's home when he already had an expensive apartment.

It was a well-known fact that the Stinky Porkster had inherited a great deal from his uncle, Mr. Finchley.

"Money is the root of all evil," replied Mom.

"For some people, life revolves around money and greed overcomes good sense.

"I am so glad for Ned. It would have been a terrible blow to him to leave his home and Boss," said Mom.

Mom loved to preach.

She was right of course. She knows her stuff, does our Mom.

I was thrilled with the outcome of the case and knew that Boss would be beside himself with joy, as would Ned.

We would get Boss's reaction from Polo when they met in the park. Polo would explain in more detail how the team attacked Rolf and what Charlotte and I had done to save the will.

Everyone would know of the role I had played in getting back the will.

I was counting on this story spreading like wildfire amongst the animal kingdom.

I had done it! Yes, I had become a Detective Cat Par Excellence!

7 Days Before Christmas

Friday Morning:

"It's time to put up our Christmas tree. I am going out to buy a Christmas tree for us to decorate," announced Mom.

We loved helping Mom hang up decorations on the tree.

She was soon back with a large tree that was carried by the corner shop owner, Mr. Rajput, who sported a large turban on his head.

Mom pulled out the box of Christmas decorations that she carefully safeguarded each January when the tree was taken down.

"Go call Monk to spend the evening with us," I whispered to Fromage.

"Decorating the Christmas tree is such fun. It will take his mind off missing his family."

So off ran Fromage and returned soon with Monk.

Mom noticed that Monk was amongst us. She remembered that Hobbs was not around and she opened an extra tin of food for Monk.

Monk polished off the food. One moment the food was there, and the next it had disappeared into Monk's belly.

Never before had he eaten at our place as he had so many treats at his home. I sometimes wondered how he could eat all the treats that he received.

He loved his food, did our pal Monk.

Hobbs and Solo tended to spoil him rotten.

Soft music floated across our cottage. We had a great deal of fun helping Mom decorate the tree.

More often than not, Fromage messed up the decorations while he played with the glass balls and got himself entangled with the brightly colored streamers.

Despite the minor mishap of Fromage breaking several glass balls and being banished to a corner over and over again, we had fun.

We decorated the tree, put up streamers, and hung bunches of mistletoe tied up in red ribbon all over the living room.

Afterwards, Mom sat down and admired our work.

Mom gave a sigh of pleasure and went off to take her bath.

Friday Evening:

The fire was crackling in the fireplace, shedding a warm glow in our comfortable sitting room.

Monk was sitting beside me watching the fire crackle, with a mournful expression on his face.

"What's wrong Monk? Are you upset about something? You're not mad that I went to see Boss by myself, are you?"

Monk's somber face turned towards me and broke into a chuckle.

"Inca, that adventure was one of the brightest moments in my life. You have turned out to be a great detective. No, Inca, even though I am worried about Terrance and my guys, it's Lance that is bugging me. He has become a nuisance."

"What is going on with him?" I asked.

Monk had not mentioned Lance's name since the day we first met him.

"Lance wants to enter me in a show," replied Monk with a look of dismay.

"A show?" I meowed in surprise.

Several of my old friends in Paris had won medals at shows. But somehow, I couldn't imagine Monk enjoying being on display.

"Have you ever been in one before, Monk? I know that there is quite a lot of work that goes into getting ready for a show."

"It's Lance's idea. He is keen on collecting the prize money," replied Monk, with a glum look on his face.

"I have a good mind to run away from home. What is horrible is that he has put me on a DIET.

"Can you imagine that? Me, on a DIET!

"Horror of horrors!" shuddered Monk, "on top of that, he brushes me every day for nearly an hour."

I dared not tell Monk that I enjoyed being brushed and that Mom dropped me off regularly at the animal spa to have a full grooming session.

"When is this show going to take place?" I meowed to quickly change the subject and avoid talking about spas.

"Tomorrow," he replied. "I have never been so insulted in my life. Who does he take me for?"

I now understood why Lance had been so keen to examine Cara and me, while he ignored Fromage.

He had wanted to enter three cats (Monk, Cara and me) in the show instead of one.

Of course, he had not been interested in Fromage as Fromage's pedigree is questionable.

But we think that Fromage's personality makes him more delightful than any pedigree in the world.

Lance may have finally abandoned his idea of entering Cara and me to the show knowing how carefully we were watched over by Mom. She could pop in at home any time of the day, unannounced.

"Chin up Monk. It will soon be over." I responded.

6 Days Before Christmas

Saturday Afternoon:

We waited eagerly for Monk. He had gone that morning with Lance for the show.

At last he arrived. He slowly ambled in, looking very pleased with himself.

Naturally we were impatient to know what had happened.

Cara begged him to start talking and he gave us a description of the day's events.

"I was woken up very early this morning," he started off.

"I had to endure one hour of brushing. Lance spent so much time examining my ears, teeth and eyes that I had no option other than to bite him a couple of times.

"That didn't stop him though.

"He *is* one bad dude!

"Finally, we got to the show. It was crowded with both humans and cats of various breeds. It was a total drag. We had to hang around for a long time.

"I longed for some sort of escape. I wouldn't have minded if:

"Lance was kidnapped by gangsters.

"The roof fell down only on Lance.

"Boss came in and attacked Lance and chased him out of London.

"A tornado whirled in and carried Lance away.

"A bus crashed into the place and headed straight for Lance so that he had to run for his life!

"Any one of the above would have been a relief.

"But nothing of the sort happened.

"What **did** happen was that many people came to look at all the contestants. They took notes, chatting away.

"I was taken out of my cage, weighed, lifted up and turned around several times. All very boring indeed.

"I looked at the other cats, some of them quite proud to be there.

"Silly spoilt brats." I thought to myself.

"Talk! Talk! Talk! That's all the humans did.

"I thought it was never going to end, this endless babbling.

"Lance tensed. The big moment had come!

"There was a hushed silence in the hall.

"Suddenly, the judge, a tall balding man stepped forward and presented me with an award and everyone clapped and cheered."

"Wow!" we said in union.

"You won, Monk?" meowed Cara clapping her paws.

"I won a ribbon all right, but Lance didn't get any prize money," crowed Monk with a smirk.

"What I won was the 'Heavyweight Champion' award - the award given to the heaviest, healthiest, sleekest cat in the show!

"I had not lost an ounce of fat! In fact, with my daily second treats at your place, thirds at Polo's, and being fed my Mrs. Applebee every day, I had actually gained weight," chuckled Monk.

"All of Lance's efforts were in vain. Serve him right!" he added with a smirk.

"The boring part though, was that the prize consisted of this ribbon, getting my photo in the newspapers and a free one-year pass to the cat spa. Can you imagine me going to the cat spa?

"Lance will be in trouble when Solo sees my face in the newspaper. He entered me in the show without talking to Solo" Monk concluded with a nasty snigger.

Monk's chuckles died down when we heard the sound of a vehicle coming to a stop near his house and doors banging.

"Looks like you have guests," I said.

Monk jumped out of the window, calling — "See you later."

For a chunky guy, he did move fast.

HEAVYWEIGHT CHAMPION

Saturday Evening:

That evening, Monk came over and tapped on our window. He told us with relief that Solo, Hobbs and Terrance had returned home safely.

Mom had received a call from Solo just as she returned home, so we had already received the news. We were waiting for Mom to jump into some warm, casual, clothes to dash over there.

More importantly, the Señora's husband had been found!

Despite Monk's joy in having his good friends back, there was also a feeling of grave concern.

Mom said that Raoul was terribly thin and could hardly walk. Other than that, he was in good health.

What was worrying was that when he fell off the mountain, he had bashed his head against a stone and could not remember anything.

Raoul had lost his memory, meaning he had amnesia.

Solo had decided not to inform the Señora about Raoul's return, as of yet. Instead he had brought Raoul directly to his house.

The doctor had examined Raoul to check on his condition. He had advised that Raoul would physically recover with nutritious food and care.

The doctor's concern was Raoul's loss of memory. He didn't recognize anyone - not Solo, not Hobbs, and not even the doctor who had treated him as a patient for many years.

Solo had called his friend Inspector Reid and Mom to come over to discuss what they should do.

How were they going to break the news to Señora?

Solo, brainy and brave as he was, was completely lost on how to deal with Señora and tell her that Raoul had amnesia and could not remember the past.

Solo, though friendly and kind, was counting on Mom to break the news to Señora.

"Chicken!!" muttered Cara, because Monk had told us that Solo disappeared when women became emotional.

5 Days Before Christmas

Sunday Morning:

When we woke up the next morning, the garden was covered in thick snow.

A winter wonderland! **Hooray!!** Last night had been the first day of winter.

This was our first snowfall and we went out to frolic and play in the snow.

Fromage suddenly bombarded us with snow balls.

"Just you wait!" Cara shouted at him as we both pounced on him.

Playing in the snow turned out to be great fun.

But Mom had to spoil the fun by insisting that we came in to dry off. Mom sure knew how to spoil our fun!

Drat & Double Drat!

Sunday Evening:

Later that day we followed Mom to Monk's house.

When we arrived, the usually silent house was bustling with activity.

The doctor had just left.

A tired looking Terrance was lying before the fire. It must have been a rough trip.

However, he was happy to see us and he stood up and wagged his tail.

"Good boy Terrance. You brought Raoul back home," said Mom as she knelt down beside him.

At that moment Solo came downstairs. He too looked exhausted but his face lit up when he saw Mom.

He came up to her and held her hands.

"I have never been so relieved to see you Missy," he said.

"Do you want to come upstairs to take a look at Raoul?

"Hobbs is preparing a light supper for us. Reid will join us later; he is at the police station right now."

We trailed behind Mom, following Solo and her up the stairs.

The room was dim but there was a soft light close to Raoul's bed. He looked very thin and drawn. There was a large bandage covering his head.

Other than that, he seemed fine to me. We left the room quietly.

During supper, Solo told Mom about what had happened in the Himalayas.

I listened to him sitting silently next to Mom.

"It was rough going," said Solo.

"Thank goodness for the guide. We never would have found this village without him. We nearly got lost in the middle of a strong windstorm when we were separated from him.

"Thanks to Terrance we were able to retrace our steps. From then on, we had a rope tied around our waists from one to the other.

"We found Raoul in a small shack. He was weak from a large head wound. The villagers had used local medicine and bandaged his head tight. Although his head injury was healing, he could not remember anything. Not even his name.

"When we came in, he was able to make some feeble comments, but he had no idea as to who we were.

"I rewarded the kind villagers. Despite their poverty, they had looked after Raoul when he stumbled into the village, hurt and weak.

"As soon as there was light we strapped Raoul onto a mule and started out on our trek back.

"The return journey was tougher. More so as the mule, with Raoul on him needed careful guidance.

"We had decided to bring four mules on the return journey. So as not to burden the mules, we kept changing Raoul from one mule to the other, even though Raoul was not that heavy.

"I was never so pleased as to be back in Kathmandu. We changed the return dates of our air tickets and brought Raoul back home.

"The doctor said that his wound had healed. But the shock of the fall would have been too strong for him. As a result, he didn't remember the past.

"Raoul needed rest and good nourishment to build up his strength. The doctor said that in a week he should be much stronger. He needed time to recover his memory."

Solo continued, "What do we say to Señora, Missy? Should we tell her immediately?"

Mom responded, "Señora left yesterday with Polo for a cure in Bath. She should be back on Christmas day. We will tell her as soon as she returns."

"Good idea, Missy," said Solo.

It was agreed that Reid and Solo would play chess with Raoul and talk to him.

Mom would visit him as well.

They would talk about all the things he loved:

- ❖ Polo,
- ❖ Horses,
- ❖ The rescue-home from where he adopted his little Polo,
- ❖ The opera music that his beloved Señora sang.

4 Days to 1 Day Before Christmas

Monday, Tuesday, Wednesday & Thursday

The last few days before Christmas were somehow blurred. I decided to lump them together in my Diary.

We visited Solo's place every day with Mom when she returned from work.

While the humans had dinner and talked together, we sat with Terrance.

I had told him of our own adventure and about forming Inca & Company to solve mysteries.

I watched his reaction anxiously.

After all, he was the true detective in the group. Would he be upset that the agency had my name on it, thereby making me the unofficial head of the group?

I guess I don't really understand dogs.

He was tickled pink!!

"Good thinking, Inca. You're a brave cat. We are going to make a good team," he said and congratulated me warmly.

Raoul now walked without a limp.

Although he remembered the events that had passed since Solo came into the shack for the first time, he still couldn't remember his past and we could see that this worried him.

He knew that he was married to a beautiful former opera singer because he had been told so. But he just could not remember her or his past.

In the meantime, Aunt Florence had come over from Provence. She was content to be among her family and old friends.

She was happy living in Provence. But she considered Mom her daughter, and thought that there was no better way to spend Christmas and New Year than with her own family.

When she heard about Raoul she was concerned for her friend. She spent time talking to him, but he did not recognize her. This was upsetting for Aunt Florence.

She remembered the fun-loving and kind Raoul of the past and couldn't quite relate to this serious, quiet man.

Christmas Day

Friday morning:

Christmas day had arrived!!!

WHOO .... PEEE!

Despite Raoul's condition, Mom and Aunt Florence were determined to make it a special day for everyone.

After all, Christmas comes but once a year!

We excitedly dashed downstairs to check out our gifts under the tree.

Fromage had received a great mound of French cheese and a spiffy new blue beret brought over for him from France by Aunt Florence.

-Ditto, for Charlotte-

For once, Mom let them have their fill of cheese.

Cara and I had received matching shawls and a bag of ping-pong balls.

We immediately started playing football with one of the balls, racing after it and knocking each other over.

"Out you go," said Mom after Fromage nearly knocked over our Christmas tree.

We rushed over to Solo's house to wish Monk and Terrance a merry Christmas.

Christmas dinner preparations were going on in full force in the kitchen.

The Applebees had taken over the catering for the Christmas party in Solo's kitchen with the help of Hobbs.

Mrs. Applebee was busy cooking up a storm for Christmas dinner. Together with Hobbs they had made a long menu of fancy-fare.

The Applebees had been thrilled to bits that Raoul had been rescued. On his return, they had rushed to introduce themselves to him. Since the Señora was away, they had taken him on a visit to his own house in the hope that he would recognize the place.

Unfortunately, this was not to be the case.

Still, Raoul was making good progress health-wise.

Solo was determined that the dinner party would go ahead despite Raoul's condition. Mom thought that the best remedy for both the Señora and Raoul was to have good friends surrounding them at this uncertain time.

Fromage had great plans for the Christmas dinner of the furry crowd. He had made his special Blue-Cheese Cake. A cherished recipe.

He had stayed up all night making it with the help of Charlotte and Monk.

Fromage insisted I included his special recipe in my Diary for future reference.

I have done so. I have added the last point about Fromage eating the lion's share as that's exactly what would happen.

Fromage's Special Blue-Cheese Cake

Ingredients:
- The ripest and strongest blue cheese stolen from our cheese shop;
- Rich Cream borrowed from Monk.

Method:
Smash the blue cheese with his paws with Charlotte doing the same;

Jump on it and lick it to keep it moist (According to Fromage that was the secret to his amazing Blue Cheese Cake);

Pour the rich cream over the smashed blue cheese;

Monk to jump on the cream and blue cheese mixture to give it a good stir;

Put the end result in one of Mom's Pyrex dishes and leave near the fire place for one whole night.

Fromage to lick his paws and those of his assistant cooks – Monk & Charlotte.

YEP, PAW Licking Good!

Share with everyone, ensuring that Fromage got the lion's share.

Cara read Fromage's recipe and wrinkled up her nose.

"You must be dreaming if you think I am going to eat your blue cheese cake," she said.

To make peace, I said that we would have other stuff to eat as well. Hobbs would make sure of that.

To appease Fromage, I said that his blue cheese cake would be the main dish of our Christmas dinner.

I needn't have bothered.

Fromage's one thought was that there was one less person to share it with.

He couldn't have cared less if Cara didn't eat his fabulous blue cheese cake.

Friday Afternoon:

The Señora came back home with Polo.

Mom and Aunt Florence went over to greet her and break the news of Raoul's return. They warned her not to be upset if he did not recognize her and explained what had happened.

The Señora broke down in tears and clung to Aunt Florence her old friend, shaking with relief and joy.

Without much ado, they walked back to Solo's house.

Of course, we followed closely behind.

Polo came back with us, yapping about his recent trip and how they had stayed in a lovely hotel where he had met many other small dogs like him.

Polo was a chatterbox.

I well imagined that he would have been very happy with the other doggies while Señora was taking her cure.

We entered Solo's house and Raoul who had been told that his wife would be brought back was slowly descending the stairs when we came in.

Polo who had been chatting away to Fromage and Charlotte about the fun time he had had and the friends he had made, suddenly stopped at the sight of Raoul.

He seemed struck dumb for a whole five seconds.

Had he lost his tongue? I wondered surprised by his silence.

There was a strange hush in the room as everyone had stopped talking.

Polo suddenly recognized Raoul as the person standing before him and went completely wild.

YAP! YAP! YAP! YAP!

Which actually meant - for those who cannot read doggie yaps:

RAOUL! RAOUL! RAOUL! RAOUL!

His little body shook with joy.

Yapping excitedly and wagging his stumpy tail non-stop, he dashed past the Señora and ran up to Raoul.

Raoul stooped down and lifted Polo in the air.

"Polo, you rascal, where have you been?" he shouted with joy.

Raoul started laughing out loud, his memory rushing back.

Everyone looked on amazed.

Polo's enthusiastic sharp yapping and evident delight at seeing his master had jolted Raoul's memory to the full.

With Polo in his arms, he rushed to the Señora who hugged him with tears running down her face.

Solo, Aunt Florence, and Mom quietly slipped out of the room to leave them alone.

Not us, of course. It was too good a scene to be missed.

There was much love and happiness in the room.

We couldn't resist watching them with delight.

Polo looked over Raoul's shoulder at us grinning from ear-to-ear.

"I have my family back together," he yapped at us happily.

Polo had the best Christmas present he could ever want.

Friday Evening:

We all met at Solo's place for dinner.

Everyone was dressed to the nines and the big dining room was all lit up.

The long table was heavily laden with all kinds of delicious food.

An enormous Christmas tree reaching up to the ceiling had been set up by Hobbs. The whole house was lit up and was all golden and warm with every fireplace in the house merrily burning bright.

We furry friends occupied the library where Monk was playing his jazz music.

Surprise, surprise! Fromage's blue cheese cake had been delicious.

Even Cara had to agree.

Of course, we had received only a tiny bit as Fromage had eaten most of it before carrying it proudly over to Monk's house.

We had eaten a special Christmas dinner prepared for us by Hobbs. We then sat down and enjoyed having a good old gossip.

Terrance had told Polo about how they had found Raoul in the distant village near the Himalayas.

Polo looked gratefully at Terrance.

"Thank you Terrance," was all he could say in a choked yap.

Terrance just wagged his tail.

Terrance is a great guy, I thought.

The emotional and serious feelings in the room suddenly transformed when there was a change of tempo in the music.

My favorite salsa music came over the air.

I looked up and saw Monk mischievously looking down at me from the stereo set that he manipulated so well.

Everyone looked at me expectantly.

"What now?" I said.

"Come on Inca!" shouted Monk.

"Dance for us!"

I tried to be modest like Terrance, but somehow it never worked for me.

I didn't need to be asked twice.

My feet twitched to the salsa beat and I felt my body swaying to the familiar music.

I threw my head back and gave one of my best performances as I danced the salsa to the beat of the rhythm humming - OLE! OLE!

My friends and family clapped in glee!

YESSS! Christmas is the most fun time of the year!!!

I hope you enjoyed reading my diary!

I Wish my 'fantastic' readers -

A Fun Christmas!

My troupe and I look forward to you reading our future adventures! Until then – We wish you A Happy, Meowy, Bow-Wowy Christmas!

R.F. Kristi invites you to free books, news and much more.

Please sign up via:

www.incabookseries.com

If you enjoyed this book, please leave a review on Amazon or Goodreads. Positive reviews help a great deal.

Thank you.

Inca Book Series:
- ☿ **The Cats Who Crossed Over from Paris**
- ☿ **Christmas Cats**
- ☿ **Cats in Provence**
- ☿ **Ninja Spy Cats**

R.F. KRISTI'S
INCA BOOK SERIES
Award-Winner in the Wishing Shelf Book Awards &
Reader's Favorite Awards

"**The Verdict:** It's pretty easy to recommend the Inca Book Series. The books are fun, interesting, and well illustrated and provide a great deal of value. The characters are fantastic and the stories are even better. The French cultural influence is a real positive for me as well because that's such a rarity and I think it's great for kids to learn about other countries and cultures. **The Illustrations:** ...The illustrations rank right up there....... The characters are all incredibly cute .... The style of these illustrations is unique. I can't think of another book we've reviewed here at Kids Fun Channel that looks anything like this. I simply love the cats, their expressions, and how much these illustrations add to the fun found in this book."

Kids Fun Channel

Connect online
www.incabookseries.com
rfkristibooks@gmail.com

The author supports the Cat Protection
Trust of Sri Lanka
https://www.facebook.com/CatProtectionTrust/

PLEASE JOIN IN SUPPORTING THE CAT
PROTECTION TRUST OF SRI LANKA